JACK HAWKSMOOR

THE CITY SHRIEKS
AT SUNDOWN.

AND JACK HAWKSMOOR
IS THE ONLY ONE WHO
CAN HEAR IT.

DUNNO. WHAT DID THE OLD LADY SAY?

LININGTON'S NEW FRIEND CAME INTO THE BUILDING ABOUT NINETY MINUTES AGO. BEEN SHOWING UP A LOT LATELY. THEY TALK POLITICS.

NOW, SEE, KEN, THAT THERE IS WHAT WE DETECTIVES CALL A CLUE.

DIE, DAVE.

SO HE BROUGHT THE FLAGS WITH HIM. PROBABLY THE MURDER WEAPON, TOO.

HE WAS IN A SUIT, WHICH WAS STRANGE...AH, AND CARRYING A LARGE SHOPPING BAG.

OH, NO. I KNOW WHAT THIS IS.

WHAT? DAVE, YOU LOOK LIKE ALL THE BLOOD JUST FELL OUT OF YOU...

CASE MY COUSIN RAN IN CHICAGO. FLAGS AT THE MURDER SITE.

CHICAGO FORENSICS I.D.'D THE MURDER WEAPON AS A HATCHET. AND THEN...

WHOA. THE COUSIN WHO GOT HIMSELF CUT UP?

NNYC; NEWS FOR NEW YORK CITY, FROM OUR STUDIOS ON THE EAST RIVER IN DOWNTOWN.

IN THIS HOUR; MAYOR GUILIANI ADDRESSES SECRECY IN GOVERNMENT, A SHOOTOUT IN CENTRAL PARK...

THERE WAS SOMETHING ELSE ODD ABOUT THE BODY THAT NAGGED HIM.

ASIDE FROM THE ADDITION OF THE FLIP-TOP HEAD.

JACK'S NOT GOOD WITH DEATH. THE PLACE MAKES HIS SKIN CRAWL.

FROM CHILDHOOD TO ADOLESCENCE, JACK WAS ABDUCTED BY PERSONS UNKNOWN TO UNDERGO A SERIES OF ORGAN IMPLANTATIONS.

EVERY TIME THEY TOOK HIM, HE THOUGHT HE WAS GOING TO DIE. EVERY TIME.

THE FIRST TIME THEY CAME, JACK WAS FIVE YEARS OLD.

IN THE MORNING, WHEN HE CHOKED OUT HIS APPALLING STORY, HIS PARENTS LAUGHED AT HIM AND HIS TERRIFIED TEARS.

BUT, OF COURSE, THEY WERE IN ON IT.

THAT'S IT. HIS TONGUE'S SITTING TOO HIGH IN THE MOUTH.

AND SOMEONE'S GOING TO WALK THROUGH THAT DOOR IN FIVE SECONDS AND JACK CAME IN THROUGH THE WINDOW IN THE HALL AND THERE'S NO WAY OUT OF THIS ROOM.

NOT DEAD. JACK WILL CALL MEDICAL ASSISTANCE FOR HIS ASSAILANT ONCE HE'S DONE.

JACK HAD ALREADY WORKED OUT THAT THAT WASN'T THE STANDARD ISSUE MORGUE ATTENDANT.

THE TONGUE WAS SITTING TOO HIGH BECAUSE THERE WAS SOMETHING UNDER IT.

ICH BIN EIN NEW YORKER

JACK'S ONLY KILLED ONCE, AND HE HATED IT.

BUT THIS HELPS.

JACK'S FINGERS TOUCH A WAD OF PAPER.

AVENUE A.

THERE'S PEOPLE IN 2010 E.
TOO MANY. PEOPLE WHO
OBVIOUSLY DIDN'T WANT
ANYBODY LOOKING AT THE
CORPSE.

JACK HAWKSMOOR IS
BEGINNING TO LOSE
HIS TEMPER.

JACK HEARS THE FRONT DOOR BANG. MUST BE OFF THE KITCHEN AREA BEYOND THAT ARCH.

FEET BANG DOWN THE STAIRCASE. SAME WEIGHT AS THE KILLER'S.

THESE PEOPLE WERE PROTECTING HIM.

BEHIND THE CLOSED DOOR, A BEDROOM -- A MAN BREATHING HEAVILY, JAMMING AN UNCOOPERATIVE CLIP INTO A VERY LARGE GUN.

ANY SECOND NOW, HE'S GOING TO LEAP OUT AND SPRAY THE ROOM. IF HE KEPT THE HANDGUN, JACK WOULD HAVE TO KILL HIM.

MICROWAVE OVENS DON'T LIKE METAL, OR PRESSURIZED LIQUIDS.

JACK HAWKSMOOR UNLAODED THE GUN WHEN SHE WASN'T LOOKING. HE DIDN'T REALLY FEEL LIKE TELLING HER.

JEAN TALKS AT A HUNDRED MILES AN HOUR. IF HAWKSMOOR CAPTURES HIM, BRINGS HIM TO JUSTICE, THERE'LL BE A MESS HE CAN'T IMAGINE.

AMERICA'S CRAZY ENOUGH WITHOUT PRODUCING THE PSYCHOPATHIC BASTARD OF ONE OF THEIR BEST-LOVED PRESIDENTS.

THERE'S A CHOPPER PREPPED FOR HIM ON THE EAST RIVER, A LINER WAITING AT SEA.

THEY NORMALLY TAKE HIM TO SKORPIOS, ARI ONASSIS' OLD ISLAND, AFTER ONE OF HIS LITTLE ESCAPADES.

HE'S KILLED CLOSE TO A HUNDRED PEOPLE, STARTING WITH A NANNY WHEN HE WAS SEVEN.

HE'S GOT TO BE AHEAD OF THEM, JEAN SAYS. PROBABLY CAUGHT A RIDE FROM AVENUE A TO THE RIVER...

SHE'S ONLY RIGHT, JACK THINKS.

THE CITY ROAD STARTS SHRIEKING AT HIM, SUBTRACTING THE WEIGHT OF THE FAMILIAR CAB AND CABBIE FROM THAT OF THE PASSENGER...

I'M *REALLY* SORRY ABOUT THIS, BUT I DON'T THINK YOU *UNDERSTAND* MUCH APART FROM GUNS.

THAT *CAB* THERE. PULL IT OVER.

PLEASE.

JENNY SPARKS

"I WAS TWENTY YEARS OLD WHEN I STOPPED AGING. EARTH STOPPED MAKING SENSE ABOUT THE SAME TIME.

"ONE MINUTE WE HAD THE SPECIAL THEORY OF RELATIVITY, AND THE NEXT, SOMEONE REWROTE THE LAWS OF PHYSICS.

"ENGLAND WAS VERY QUIETLY TOUCHED BY THE *STRANGE*. I WAS THERE TO SEE THE *SHIFTSHIPS* WHEN THE *DOOR* APPEARED.

"I WAS A *GIRL*. I THREW MYSELF INTO THE TROUBLE THAT *FOLLOWED* THE DOOR, FOUGHT THE KING OF NAILS FROM SLIDING ALBION AND SLEPT WITH BEAUTIFUL BLUE-SKINNED PRINCES...

"THE TWENTIES WERE AN AGE OF *SCIENTIFIC ROMANCE*.

"I *LOVED* IT.

THAT'S YOUR LOT, BOSS MOSELEY!

THERE'LL BE A WAR YET— OOF!

NOT WITH YOU IN JAIL AND THE WORKERS TAKING CONTROL OF YOUR CORRUPT MUNITIONS FACTORY!

HOW DID YOU KNOW?

EASY, CLARENCE— WHERE YOU AND YOUR REPORTER'S INSTINCT GO, TROUBLE FOLLOWS!

I LOVE YOU, JENNY! LET'S GO TO BED!

DO I LOOK DESPERATE TO YOU?

"WE SPRANG OVER THOSE IMPRISONED DEPRESSION STREETS, ME AND MINE; LIKE OUR LIVES WERE BEING WRITTEN BY TEENAGE KIDS, AND ALL THEIR GUTS AND LUNACY AND HOPE WERE ENCODED INTO EVERY PIECE OF US.

"I STAYED THROUGH THE *FORTIES*. IN RETROSPECT, PROBABLY A BAD IDEA."

"I COULD'VE GONE WITH NO ONE THE WISER; NO ONE REALLY BELIEVED IN US. WE WERE URBAN MYTHS."

Bring in Clarence Cornwall...

"BUT I WAS HOOKED ON THE IDEA OF *MAKING THINGS BETTER*."

SPARKS! Y'LOOK AWFUL!

YOU GOT HIM?

SURE! HE'S IN THE INTERVIEW ROOM--

EMPTY IT. I WANT HIM ALONE.

OH, FOR-- OKAY, SPARKS, OKAY.

AND LISTEN, HAVE YOU BEEN FOOLING AROUND WITH MY SON ALAN? I--NEVER MIND...

HI, JENNY.

WHY, CLARENCE?

HOW DOES THE CITY'S BEST REPORTER GET INVOLVED IN A PLOT TO RELEASE ZYKLON B GAS INTO THE CITY ORPHANAGE?

IT'S FULL OF BLACK KIDS.

THAT'S IT?

THAT'S IT.

"BUT I DON'T THINK AMERICA REALLY *WANTED* TO BE BETTER, BACK THEN.

SO NONE OF THIS GETS REPORTED BACK TO THE STATES?

UH-UH. I KEEP THIS ALL TO MYSELF. I HAVE MY *OWN* AGENDA, AS THE GENERAL *KNOWS.*

GOT TO SAY, THOUGH, THIS IS A SWEET DEAL.

STILL DOESN'T *SIT* RIGHT WITH ME. USING THE SPACE GROUP AS A COVER STORY...

THAT'S YOUR SIXTEENTH GLASS, COLONEL SPARKS.

I DIDN'T REALIZE YOU WERE *COUNTING,* GENERAL. *KIND* OF YOU.

YOU'D RATHER THE BRITISH PEOPLE WERE *INFORMED* THAT AGENTS OF A *PARALLEL* WORLD--

--INCLUDING AN ENGLAND RULED BY *SICILIAN PRINCES*--

--HAVE BEEN RUNNING AROUND THE COUNTRYSIDE SINCE THE *TWENTIES,* THEIR TRACKS *WIPED* BY YOUR *GOVERNMENT*--

AAAOOOOO

WHAT THE HELL IS THAT *NOISE?*

:*splurf*:

INCURSION ALARM!

"THE *HELICARS* WERE OUR BIG *P.R.* GIMMICK -- 'SCIENCE FICTION IS SCIENCE TODAY!' AND ALL THAT GUFF."

"WE HAD TO DO *SOMETHING* TO COVER FOR SLIDING ALBION'S SHIFTSHIPS STILL MOVING IN BRITISH AIRSPACE."

"ANYTHING OTHER THAN TELL THE *TRUTH*."

OH, THANK GOD YOU'RE *BACK*--

WHAT'S THE STORY, BILL?

WE JUST GOT A *MESSAGE CAPSULE* SHOT THROUGH THE SHIFTDOOR WE KEEP HERE AT HQ--

--SLIDING ALBION IS AT WAR WITH SLIDING *EUROPE*.

WE'RE STARING DOWN THE BARREL OF *PARALLEL WORLD WAR ONE*.

I HEARD THAT. WHAT'S THE *PROJECTION?*

THEY'LL GO TO *BACTERIAL WEAPONRY* FIRST. WE PRESUME THEY'LL SHUT THE SHIFTDOORS TO CONSERVE ENERGY...

...IT'LL ALL BE OVER IN A FEW HOURS...

"AND THERE IT ALL WENT.

"I STILL DREAMED OF GETTING ON EQUAL TERMS WITH SLIDING ALBION; BRINGING THEIR TECHNOLOGY HERE.

"THE WORLD WE COULD HAVE MADE.

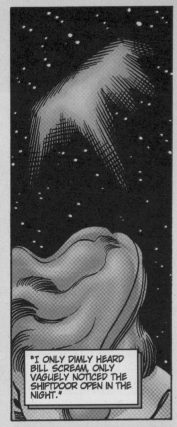

"I ONLY DIMLY HEARD BILL SCREAM, ONLY VAGUELY NOTICED THE SHIFTDOOR OPEN IN THE NIGHT."

WE GUESSED ALBION WAS DESPERATELY TRYING TO SAVE THEIR LONDON FROM A BACTERIAL ATTACK.

"SEEING IT COMING, THEY OPENED A MASSIVE SHIFTDOOR AND VENTED IT *HERE.*

"IT DIDN'T SAVE THEM; THEIR DYING ACT WAS ONE OF CONTEMPT FOR US."

OH, HELL...

JENNY? IT'S JANOS... JENNNNNY...

HEY, CHECK OUT THE GUY IN THE GREEN.

I'M FEELING THE IRRESISTIBLE URGE TO LAY DOWN...

JANOS? THIS BETTER BE GOOD, YOU'VE MADE ME GET SMOKE IN MY EYE.

YOU'RE SUPPOSED TO BREATHE IT IN, NOT LOOK AT IT... LISTEN, YOU SEEN ABEL?

ABOUT TWENTY MINUTES AGO. SOME BIKERS WERE SODDING ABOUT WITH SYRINGES, TALKING ABOUT PINNING PEOPLE DOWN AND SHOOTING THEM UP.

ABEL WENT TO SORT THEM OUT, HIS USUAL MACHO CAVEMAN CRAP. WHY?

WELL, HE WAS SUPPOSED TO MEET ME BACK HERE TO DEAL WITH THE NEWS PEOPLE, AND--

HOLD IT. I JUST SAW THE BIKERS.

LOOKING DISTINCTLY UNBRUISED, JANOS.

AAAARRRR

"I COULDN'T WAIT FOR THE OTHERS. EACH SECOND SAW ANOTHER TWENTY PEOPLE DEAD.

"ALL I COULD DO WAS REACH OUT FOR THE *STAGE GENERATORS* --"

"IT STARTED GOING WRONG WHEN THE *BABIES* DISAPPEARED.

"I WAS WITH THE PEOPLE WHO WERE *KIDS* WHEN THE *VENT* HAPPENED.

"BY THE EIGHTIES, THEY'D GROWN UP WEIRD AND HUNGRY.

"THEY SAW WHAT WE MISSED IN THE SIXTIES. THEY WANTED TO TRY IT FOR THEMSELVES.

"I'D SEEMED THE CLEAN ONE OF THE SIXTIES GROUP, SO THEY CAME TO ME.

"WE HAD THATCHER'S *GOVERNMENT* TERRIFIED. WE WERE STICKING OUR NOSES IN EVERYTHING, LOOKING FOR THE BEST WAY TO MAKE A DIFFERENCE.

WELL, WE'VE SODDED THIS *RIGHT* UP, HAVEN'T WE?

YOU KNOW WHAT KIND OF CRAP YOU'LL CATCH AT SCOTLAND YARD FOR BRINGING US IN, INSPECTOR BULSTRODE?

UNTIL YOU JUST TOLD ME THAT, I DIDN'T GIVE A TOSS.

BUT NOW I FIND OUT THAT ONE OF *YOUR PEOPLE* WAS IN THE *AREA?* NOT IMPRESSED, SPARKS.

ME NEITHER.

HAS FIRESIGN STILL GOT HIS MOBILE PHONE SWITCHED OFF?

YES. LOOK, JUST BECAUSE HE WAS OVER HAMMERSMITH, DOESN'T *MEAN*--

YES IT BLOODY DOES!

I'VE TOLD YOU TIME AND *BLOODY* TIME *AGAIN*-- YOU SODDING WELL *WATCH OUT* FOR THE *NORMAL* PEOPLE!

BECAUSE *THEY'RE* MORE IMPORTANT THAN WE ARE, *YOU VAIN AND SELF-OBSESSED SODDING TOERAGS!*

GOD ALMIGHTY.

THIS IS NUMBER SIX, RIGHT, BULSTRODE? SIX BABIES ABDUCTED, THEIR SINGLE MOTHERS KILLED.

CORRECT.

I'M GOING TO FIND FIRESIGN.

YOU DO WHAT YOU WANT.

"FIRESIGN AND HIS WIFE HAD A NICE FLAT -- APARTMENT, SORRY -- IN WEST LONDON.

"HIS REAL NAME WAS MATT AND HE WORKED IN THE STOCK EXCHANGE BY DAY. SHE DID CHARITY WORK. VERY TRENDY. VERY RICH.

"THEY WERE ALWAYS UP LATE. LEFT LIGHTS ON IN THEIR FLAT.

"GETTING IN WAS EASY.

"I WAS IN THEIR SPARE BEDROOM; I'D STAYED HERE BEFORE. IT WAS A BIG ENOUGH PLACE THAT THEY BARELY NOTICED VISITORS.

"I HEARD VOICES. I DIDN'T LIKE THEM."

...KNOW, I KNOW, BUT IT'S GOT TO STOP.

IF YOU COULD ONLY SEE HER FACE...

YOU HEARD HIM ON THE PHONE JUST NOW. JENNY DOESN'T LIKE IT.

YEAH, WELL, I COULDN'T GIVE A DAMN WHAT JENNY LIKES.

WHAT I'M SAYING IS, IF SHE FINDS OUT, WE'RE DEAD, OKAY? JUST DEAD.

FIND OUT *WHAT?*

YOU WERE SPOTTED FLYING OVER HAMMERSMITH TONIGHT, MATT.

REALLY.

YOU'RE TAKING THE CHILDREN, AREN'T YOU, MATT?

YES. YES, I AM.

KILL HER.

KILL HER!

STOP! YOUR GODDAMN BULLETS WILL GO THROUGH THE GODDAMN WALL --

OWWW

BATTALION

11:55 AM.

THOUGHT I MIGHT GRAB SOME LUNCH, LOOK AROUND...

...VEGETATE IN PUBLIC...

HA! IF YOU'RE RESORTING TO SARCASM, THEN I KNOW I'VE WON.

SEE YOU IN THE MORNING, JACKSON.

WEATHERMAN OUT.

IS THAT WHO I *THINK* IT IS?

I KNOW WHO *YOU* THINK IT IS.

THAT WAS A *BAD PICTURE* IN *REVERE'S BUGLE.* THAT PSIONIC *AMPLIFICATION SUIT* BATTALION WEARS INTERFERES WITH *CAMERA FILM.*

THAT'S *HIM,* FUZZY PICTURE OR NO.

THAT'S *BATTALION.* STORMWATCH'S FAVORITE SON.

IT'S *ME.* WE'VE GOT A *PROBLEM.* THERE'S A STORMWATCH OFFICER *RIGHT HERE.*

ABORT --

HEY. IT MIGHT NOT *BE* A PROBLEM. IT MIGHT BE A *BLESSING.* A SIGN.

HE AIN'T *WEARING* HIS AMPLIFICATION SUIT. THE BUGLE SAID HE *NEEDS* IT FOR HIS *POWERS* TO WORK PROPERLY.

YOU WANTED TO SEND A *MESSAGE* TODAY. WELL, THERE IT *IS.*

A *STORMWATCH* MAN. LARGE AS *LIFE,* AND *BLACK AS THE ACE OF SPADES* TO BOOT.

CAN YOU HEAR ME?

QUITE A CRACK ON THE HEAD YOU TOOK.

YOU ARE THE PRISONER OF *MAMBA TEAM MILITIA*, MR. BATTALION.

MY NAME IS *McCREARY*, COMMANDING OFFICER. MY MEN MADE A *PRESENT* OF YOU.

...HOW LONG HAVE I BEEN OUT?

I CAN HEAR A METAL DOOR OPENING, GRINDING... MUST BE THE *GARAGE'S* MAIN DOOR...

WE'RE ONLY JUST LEAVING.

REST MY EYES. JUST FOR A MOMENT.

NO! SHUT YOUR EYES NOW, YOU'LL WAKE UP *DEAD.*

LISTEN. JUDGE THE VAN'S *SPEED.* MEMORIZE THE *TURNS* AND *STOPS.*

HEAD HURTS. CAN'T CONCENTRATE ENOUGH TO TRIGGER MY *POWERS...*

LEFT TURN. MMM... TWENTY YARDS. RIGHT TURN. RIGHT TURN *AGAIN.*

HUNDRED YARDS? *STOP.* LEFT TURN. *THIRTY...* SLOW... *STOP.*

MY GOD. THE BASTARDS ARE WITHIN ONE HUNDRED *YARDS* OF THE *TARGET.*

OKAY... REST JUST FOR A *SECOND...*

A *SECOND,* HE SAYS.

A SECOND MIGHT BE ALL I *HAVE.* CAN'T SEE THE *TIMER.*

WHEN STORMWATCH *BEGAN,* IT WAS INTENDED TO OPERATE *PUBLICLY.* AN OPEN ORGANIZATION.

BUT THE *WEATHERMAN* ARGUED FOR WHAT HE CALLED *SEQUESTRATION.*

SO, YEAH, IT'S PUBLIC KNOWLEDGE THAT I USE AMPLIFICATION FOR MY TELEKINESIS IN COMBAT.

IT'S NOT PUBLIC KNOWLEDGE THAT MY TELEKINESIS IS ACTUALLY PRETTY USEFUL WITHOUT AMPLIFICATION.

POCKET'S EMPTY. THEY TOOK THE *FETISH.* SO THAT'S *ONE* OPTION GONE. AND I DON'T HAVE MY *CYBER-TRAN SUIT* ON.

AND MY RATHER IRRESPONSIBLE NAP HAS LET MY *HEAD* GET *UNSCRAMBLED.*

I CAN'T DO THE *BIG* STUFF WITHOUT *AMPING.*

BUT TELEKINESIS IS ALL ABOUT MOVING THINGS, AND CAN BE JUST AS EFFECTIVE ON THE *SMALL* SCALE.

OH, MAN.

LESS THAN A MINUTE.

HOME-MADE BOMB. DON'T EXPECT THE DEVICE TO MAKE SENSE.

REACH *IN*, REACH FOR THE SMALLEST *PARTS* OF IT, FOR THE *ELECTRICITY* --

-- *STOP* EVERYTHING *MOVING*, STOP THE *POWER* FLOWING --

END OF THE STREET, THEN RIGHT, THEN RIGHT AGAIN.

THEY MUST BE GETTING *NERVOUS.* THEY DIDN'T HEAR A BLAST. AND THEY CAN'T *RAISE* THEIR *OBSERVERS* THERE ON THE RADIO.

CAN'T CALL THE POLICE AND RISK A *SIEGE.*

CAN'T CALL SKYWATCH WITHOUT THE *FETISH.*

THIS ONE'S ALL DOWN TO *ME.*

NOTHING. I SAY WE GET *OUT.*

...AGREED. START THE ENGINE. WE DUMP THE CAR AT THE EDGE OF TOWN AND SPLIT UP.

I DON'T *GET* IT. THE BOMB WAS SO SIMPLE IT WAS *FOOLPROOF.*

THE FEDS PROBABLY AIMED SOME KIND OF *ELECTRICITY-KILLING RAY* AT IT. HAVE YOU SEEN ANY *BLACK HELICOPTERS* TODAY?

THEY ALWAYS MOVE IN *BLACK HELICOPTERS.*

555-PIG

HURK

HEART...

I MANAGED TO FIND MY FETISH, AND CALLED IN TO THE WEATHERMAN.

THE POLICE WERE GOOD ABOUT IT, REALLY.

MCCREARY LIVED LONG ENOUGH TO STAND TRIAL. STORMWATCH DIDN'T WANT HIM, AND SO HE WENT TO REGULAR PRISON INSTEAD OF A CRYOGENIC LOCKTANK.

HE DIED THERE A FEW MONTHS LATER. HEART DAMAGE.

THE BOMB-MAKING EQUIPMENT WAS FOUND, OF COURSE, AND THE STACKS OF WEIRD LITERATURE. NO ONE WAS IN ANY DOUBT OF THE TRUTH ABOUT MAMBA TEAM.

BUT MY UNCLE HAD TO LEAVE TOWN ANYWAY.

AND THE REPRESENTATIVE FROM CONSTITUTION, ALABAMA, TODAY INTRODUCED A BILL TO BAR U.N. OFFICERS FROM ACTING ON AMERICAN SOIL.

ROSE TATTOO

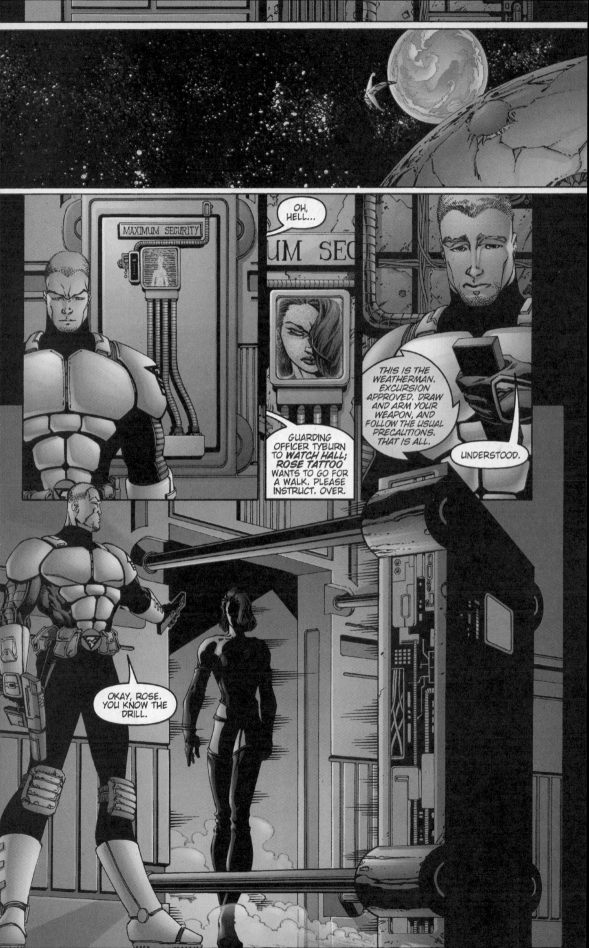

LEAD THE WAY, ROSE.

ROSE. WALK ON.

I MEAN IT.

ROSE, DAMMIT, YOU KNOW I'M UNDER ORDERS FROM THE WEATHERMAN TO SHOOT YOU IF --

MPH

HMMMF

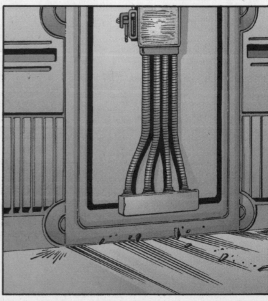

BLOODY HELL! IT'S BASTARD *FREEZING!* WINTER, IF THERE'S NOT A BAR HERE LIKE YOU *PROMISED,* I'M GOING TO DO YOU --

JENNY, I *TOLD* YOU. IT'S *NIKOLAS.*

THE WEATHERMAN HAS CONTRIVED TO KEEP THE THREE STORMWATCH UNITS *APART* FOR SO LONG THAT I'VE ONLY GOTTEN TO KNOW SOME OF YOU IN *BATTLE.*

TONIGHT WE DRINK TOGETHER AND LEARN TOGETHER. AND IT'S *FIRST* NAMES.

AND THERE *IS* A BAR, RIGHT *HERE.*

IT'S CALLED *THE LAST SHOT.*

UNDERGROUND NUCLEAR TESTS ARE PERFORMED NEAR HERE, FOR RELIGIOUS PURPOSE. I'M TOLD THE U.N. KNOWS ABOUT IT, BUT TURNS A BLIND EYE.

NUKES FOR *RELIGION?*

SCIENTISTS IN CITY 57, SO THE STORY GOES, ESTABLISHED THAT THE *HUMAN SOUL* IS AN *ELECTROMAGNETIC FIELD.*

IT'S SAID THAT THEY FURTHER ESTABLISHED WHERE SOULS *GO* --

-- SIX OF THE WAKE BEERS, PLEASE --

-- THAT *HEAVEN* AND *HELL* ARE NOTHING BUT *SIEGE ENGINES,* STRAINING AGAINST EACH OTHER, AND THAT *SOULS* PROVIDE THEIR *MOTIVE POWER.*

THE LAST SHOT IS A BAR FOR THE PEOPLE WHO WISH TO *CHEAT* HEAVEN AND HELL OF THEIR SOULS.

FOR *ELECTROMAGNETIC FIELDS* ARE TERMINALLY *DISRUPTED* BY NUCLEAR BLASTS.

THEY TAKE THEIR LAST DRINK HERE, BEFORE BEING STRAPPED TO AN UNDERGROUND NUCLEAR DEVICE BY SYMPATHETIC TECHNICIANS.

THESE *PHOTOS; THESE* ARE THE PEOPLE WHO CHEATED GOD AND THE DEVIL.

TO THE TRIUMPHANT DEAD.

OH, COME **ON.** ~SHULP~ I THOUGHT YOU'D **APPRECIATE** A LITTLE LOCAL HISTORY.

NO OFFENSE, **NIKOLAS** -- BUT YOU'RE A **BASKET CASE.**

VICTORIA, ISN'T IT? WELL, WHY AM I A BASKET CASE?

YOU TAKE US OUT FOR A FRIENDLY DRINK TO THE LAST PORT FOR SOME WEIRDO CULT THAT LIKES STRAPPING THEMSELVES TO **NUKES?**

I SHUDDER TO THINK WHERE YOU'D TAKE A **WOMAN** OUT TO. CHERNOBYL? RWANDA?

SHE HAS A **POINT** THERE, NICK. IT DOES HAVE TO BE SAID THAT THE LAST TIME YOU GOT LAID, **GORBACHEV** WAS IN POWER...

NIGEL, YOU HAVE THOUGHT OF NOTHING BUT SEX AND ALCOHOL SINCE YOU MUTATED INTO THAT SENTIENT **GASEOUS** FORM.

IT'S SAD THAT YOU CAN NO LONGER... **OPERATE** LIKE A NORMAL HUMAN, BUT --

AA, WELL. *THAT'S* WHERE YOU'RE *WRONG.*

ME AND THE SKYWATCH *MEDICAL* TEAM, WE'VE BEEN THINKING THIS *THROUGH.*

I'M A BIG BUNCH OF *ELECTRIFIED GAS,* BUT I *CAN* DRINK, AND I CAN GET *DRUNK.*

AND NOT TOO LONG AGO, TABOO *KICKED* ME IN THE *UNMENTIONABLES,* RIGHT? *HURT* LIKE HELL. WHICH SHOULDN'T BE *POSSIBLE,* SINCE I'M GAS AND ALL.

TURNS OUT WHAT KEEPS ME TOGETHER IS A LOW-POWER *FORCE FIELD.* I'M LEARNING TO *MANIPULATE* THAT.

BUT --

AND MY *ELECTRICAL SYSTEM* BEHAVES A BIT LIKE A *NERVOUS* SYSTEM. DOCS RECKON IT'S A BIT PSYCHOSOMATIC, BUT THERE YOU GO. I CAN *FEEL.*

ANYWAYS A FEW WEEKS BACK, I'M DOWN AT CLARK'S BAR, AND THERE'S SOME *SUPERHERO GROUPIES* HANGING AROUND. AND ONE OF THEM, AA, SHE WAS *GORGEOUS,* SHE WAS...

YOU *DIDN'T.*

TURNS OUT I *CAN,* SO I DID.

FOR *HOURS.*

THAT'S *DISGUSTING.*

IT'S BLOODY *BEAUTIFUL.* I CAN GROW IT RIGHT OUT OF ME LIKE -- WELL, SEE, D'YOU WANT TO HAVE A *LOOK?*

NO!

HENRY BENDIX; WEATHERMAN (COMMANDING OFFICER) OF STORMWATCH, UNITED NATIONS SPECIAL CRISIS INTERVENTION UNIT

MIND WRITER SOFTWARE SELECTED; ACCEPTING DICTATION DIRECTLY FROM CEREBRUM.

The three StormWatch units are now settled in their posts. The Special Security Council remains quiet. The time approaches.

I want to change the world. I now have the tools for the job and the space in which to work.

Mark this file as ABOVE TOP SECRET and save it in my locked memory tower. Private record begins:

I believe I have the support where it counts. StormWatch Prime accept my authority unquestioningly.

StormWatch Red remain confused but compliant (with the exception of Rose Tattoo), which is an acceptable state for human weapons.

I wait only for the first opportunity. The clock starts now.

There's never been anyone like me before.

StormWatch Black loathe authority, but perceive me as the lesser evil.

Rose Tattoo will kill for the sake of killing. It is who she is. Thankfully, the others remain ignorant of her origins.

NIGEL, *PLEASE*, I'D LIKE SOME FOOD TO SOAK UP THE ALCOHOL A LITTLE, SINCE YOU *INSIST* WE ALL KEEP UP WITH YOUR DRINKING...

THEY MAKE SAUSAGES OUT OF HORSE'S RINGPIECES!

I SAID NO. NO *WAY* I'M ORDERING FOOD IN FRANCE, AND THAT'S *IT*.

AH. AN *IRISHMAN*.

AW, JAYSUS... HE SPEAKS ENGLISH...

HE *DOES*. AND IF OUR FOOD IS NOT GOOD ENOUGH FOR AN... *IRISHMAN*... THEN I'M SURE WE CAN WARM SOME *PEAT* FOR YOUR DINNER.

AA, SO IT'S LIKE *THAT*, IS IT NOW? YOU WANT TO STEP *OUTSIDE* WI' ME AND BE SAYING THAT, WEE LAD?

...*RINGPIECES*? I DON'T THINK OUR HORSES IN TIBET *HAVE* THOSE, NIGEL...

VICKY, YOUR FRENCH IS BETTER THAN MINE. I'VE FOUND THIS *GOD* HERE, AND HE'S TRYING TO *TELL* ME SOMETHING...

UNITED NATIONS SPECIAL
CRISIS INTERVENTION UNIT,
INCIDENT LOG #0012087

The germ of the
incident was first
detected here, upon
the SkyWatch
orbital platform.

Although, according to
protocol, StormWatch is
not supposed to act
unless Code Perfect is
invoked by a government
holding United Nations
membership, you will
see that my actions
were necessary.

I take full
responsibility
for the loss of
life and other
damages incurred
by my actions.

From the platform's Watch Hall, anomalous events the world over can be detected and analyzed.

The operator at desk twenty-three initiated a yellow alert at 0423 Central European Time.

Unusual electromagnetic radiation had begun to emit, in a focused way reminiscent of a leak in a dam, from a remote part of Serbia.

The usual communications were made to the Serbian government. They garnered no reply.

I chose to activate a six-person StormForce unit to investigate. This is within my boundaries as StormWatch commanding officer.

The unit was duly transferred to the forest location in question.

At 0644, Transfer Bay Two initiated emergency teleportation retrieval at my order and recovered one member of the StormForce unit.

That officer remains in the psychiatric wing of the SkyWatch Medical Deck. He is not expected to regain mental stability, and will remain in our care until his natural death.

Further overtures to the Serbian government were greeted with obfuscation and nervousness. Negotiations took several hours.

By 1520, I had received a communication from yourselves requesting clarification of the situation, following complaints by the Serbs.

The radiative emmissions grew stronger.

During this waiting period, I obtained history and data on the location in question.

It was removed from maps in 1655. The story behind this is sparse and dubious.

There are tales of plague, of strange lights emanating from underground, of rooms taking on new angles and driving the inhabitants insane.

A pamphlet from 1660 purports to tell the story of a priest, who escaped to the nearest town with terrible sores and wounds upon his person.

He saw women, who wore reptilian hide beneath their human skin, seducing the menfolk and bearing children underground.

Awful children.

At 1755, I brought
SkyWatch from
yellow alert to
Police Position and
activated StormWatch.

I broke from the usual
practice of activating
one of the three
specialized StormWatch
teams...

STORMWATCH PRIME:
major superhuman threats
STORMWATCH BLACK:
covert insertion/urban conflict
STORMWATCH RED:
destructive/deterrent acts

...and instead assembled
a composite group for
maximal effectiveness
in the face of an
unknown threat.

WINTER:
Nikolas Kamarov
energy absorption/redirection
FIELD LEADER

FUJI:
Toshiro Misawa
Sentient gaseous
POSTHUMAN
enhanced strength

FAHRENHEIT:
Lauren Pennington
firestarter
FIELD DEPUTY

HELLSTRIKE:
Nigel Keane
sentient gaseous
POSTHUMAN
superheated plasma
projection

FLINT:
Victoria Ojuku
resistant to damage/
enhanced strength

At this point in my report, I choose to incorporate the mission's communication logs.

WINTER: SKYWATCH FROM WINTER. WE'RE FACING WHAT LOOKS TO BE AN ENTRANCE PORT SET IN THE FOREST FLOOR. NO SIGN OF THE ANALYSIS TEAM.

FUJI: NOTE THE RIM OF THE PORT. RUST. THIN SHAVINGS OF METAL LEFT FROM WHEN THE DOOR OPENED. THIS IS VERY OLD.

HELLSTRIKE: SILLY BASTARDS MUST'VE GONE INSIDE. HAVE THEY NOT SEEN ANY BLOODY HORROR FILMS? I MEAN, YOU DON'T GO INSIDE...

HELLSTRIKE: I **SAID**, YOU **DON'T** GO INSIDE...

FLINT: DOES ANYONE HAVE THE **FAINTEST** IDEA WHAT THIS **IS**? BECAUSE, YOU KNOW, I'M JUST **LOST**...

FAHRENHEIT: THE LIGHT IN HERE SEEMS TO BE COMING FROM MOLD GROWING IN THE WALLS' CONTOURS. ALTHOUGH THERE DOES ALSO SEEM TO BE ELECTRICAL POWER INVOLVED...

WINTER: CONFIRM THAT. I CAN **FEEL** IT MOVING BEHIND THE WALLS, LIKE UNDERGROUND STREAMS...

WINTER: THIS PLACE IS MASSIVE, AND... THE **DIMENSIONS** FEEL ALL WRONG. CRUSHING, DOMINATING. DOESN'T FEEL LIKE IT WAS BUILT FOR **PEOPLE**.

At 0620, StormWatch found the second of the six analysis team members. He was quite dead.

It was unclear whether the vegetable growth in his excavated gut had killed him through a violent excursion, or whether his corpse had been used as a post-mortem incubator for it.

Later analysis could not match the plant to any known flora, or even place it within a known genus. It's origin and nature remains a mystery.

HELLSTRIKE: HE TURNED THE POOR BLEEDER INTO A SHAGGIN' WINDOWBOX, SO HE DID...

The communication logs capture the distinctive sound of Hellstrike's superhuman ability to project high-velocity jets of superheated plasma.

The noises that follow accompanied the incineration of flesh, the delinquence of vital organs, and the ignition of expanding internal gases within the creature.

I mention all this because the Special Security Council has frequently complained of the lack of detail contained in my reports.

I trust that there will be no further messages on this point.

WINTER: ...WE'VE ENTERED WHAT LOOKS TO BE A CENTRAL HALL.

WINTER: IT'S UNLIT. NO POWER HERE. NO IMMEDIATE SIGNS OF OPERATING MACHINERY THAT MIGHT ACCOUNT FOR THE DETECTED EMISSIONS.

FAHRENHEIT: DOESN'T HAVE TO BE. ALLIGATOR-BOY BACK THERE WAS ROTTEN WITH THE SAME RADIATION, RIGHT?

FAHRENHEIT: SO MAYBE IT'S BIOLOGICALLY GENERATED AND... OH, MAN... WOULD YOU LOOK AT THAT...

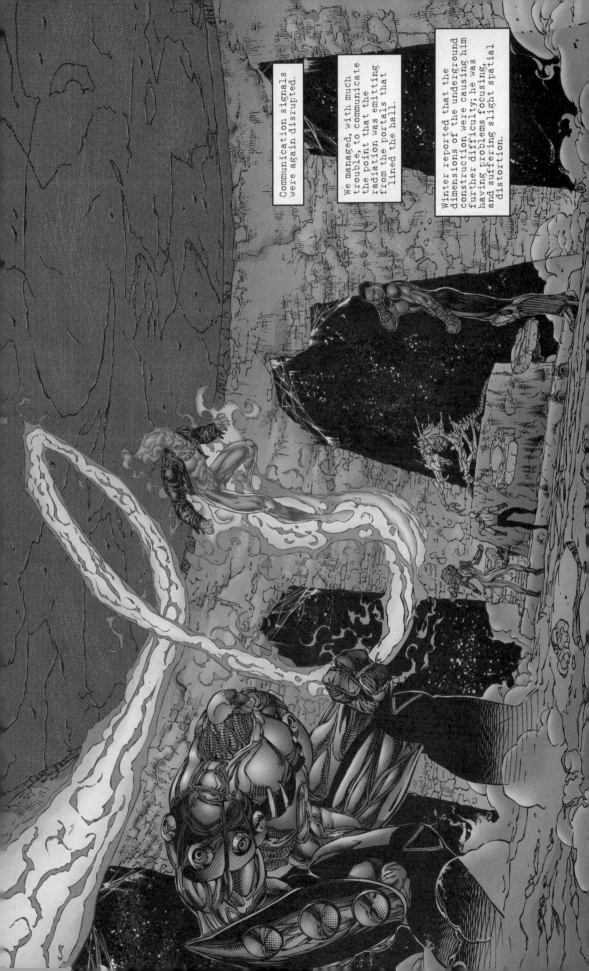

Communication signals were again disrupted.

We managed, with much trouble, to communicate to the point that the radiation was emitting from the portals that lined the hall.

Winter reported that the dimensions of the underground construction were causing him further difficulty; he was having problems focusing, and suffering slight spatial distortion.

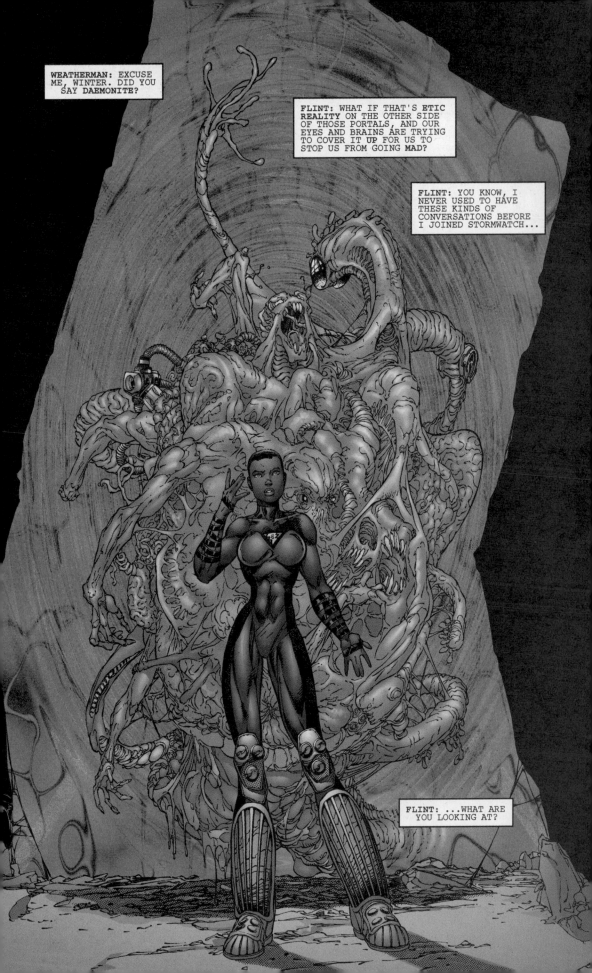

StormWatch had had previous experience with Daemonites, as well as their blood rivals, the Kheran species. Daemonites are an extra-terrestrial race.

They had been at war with Khera for millenia; a battle that had progressed far beyond their home planets, and even their home solar systems. By the time they found earth, it was their silently agreed policy to make war on soils not their own.

They found Earth several hundred years ago. They used us as shields, as breeding stock, as tools... and, it seems, as experimental animals.

Those old documents were trying to warn us. Four hundred years ago, Daemonites constructed an experimental station beneath this remote woodland, and began obtaining human seed and corpses for their task.

It would appear obvious that that task was to engineer some form of near-mindless biological military device from human genetic material.

And then...what? Were the Daemonites murdered by Kheran troops? Did they have warning and so dropped their once-human creations into a special hiding place?

Today, centuries later, perhaps some insulation perished, allowing the portal's weird radiations to be detected. And when the analysis team breached the station -- did that wake them, behind those doors?

They were doubtless programmed to kill all intruders, no matter what their species were. If the long-dead village nearby had stormed the station, then these creatures would have blithely destroyed their own parents.

FUJI: AND THEY WON'T GIVE US THE TIME TO TRY AND COMMUNICATE, TO TELL THEM THAT ALL THE DAEMONITES ON EARTH ARE DEAD... ALL WE CAN DO IS KILL THEM SO THAT WE WILL SURVIVE...

FLINT: JUST COOK THE DAMN THINGS **OFF** ME BEFORE THEY **GROW** SOMETHING THAT'LL **PIERCE** MY **SKIN** -- GO **ON**, YOU **CAN'T BURN** ME, LAUREN --

WINTER: WEATHERMAN FROM WINTER -- **MORE** OF THESE PORTALS ARE OPENING UP. I'M TRYING TO ABSORB AS MUCH OF THE AMBIENT **RADIATION** AS **POSSIBLE**...

WINTER: EVERYBODY **BACK OFF.** IF THESE PORTALS ARE CONTAINMENT CELLS OF SOME KIND, AND THE RADIATION IS LEAKING FROM THEM, AND NOW THESE THINGS CAN GET OUT...

WINTER: ...THEN IT'D MAKE A DEGREE OF SENSE THAT THIS RADIATION I'M ABSORBING HAS A HAND IN KEEPING THEM UNDER CONTROL.

WINTER: I'M GOING TO AMPLIFY AND RELEASE IT AT THEM -- AS LONG AS I DON'T PASS OUT FROM STARING AT THIS DAMNED PORTAL --

Winter is a soldier; his background is with the Russian Spetznaz, crack troops analogous to the Navy Seals of Delta Force, with one exception. Spetznaz are more clever and frankly much, much scarier.

They don't let things like death and encroaching insanity get in the way of doing the job.

In summary, then: a four hundred year old time bomb went off in Serbia that day. We were touched by things from beyond space, things grown from our own meat and juices.

God knows how many more such time bombs await us in the future. Our world holds too many secrets, and too many of those secrets are lethal to us.

I would once more impress upon the Special Security Council that only one thing in this mined world stands between us and them.

StormWatch.

END

GALLERY

Issue #43 Cover by
Tom Raney
and
Randy Elliott

Issue #44 Cover by
Tom Raney
and
Randy Elliott

DON'T BE
A *FOOL! RUN*
FOR YOUR
LIFE!

Issue #44
Variant Cover by
Mark Irwin

Issue #44
Variant Cover by
Gil Kane

Issue #45 Cover by
Tom Raney
and
Randy Elliott

Issue #46 Cover by
Tom Raney
and
Randy Elliott

Issue #47 Cover by
Jim Lee
and
Tom Raney

GALLERY

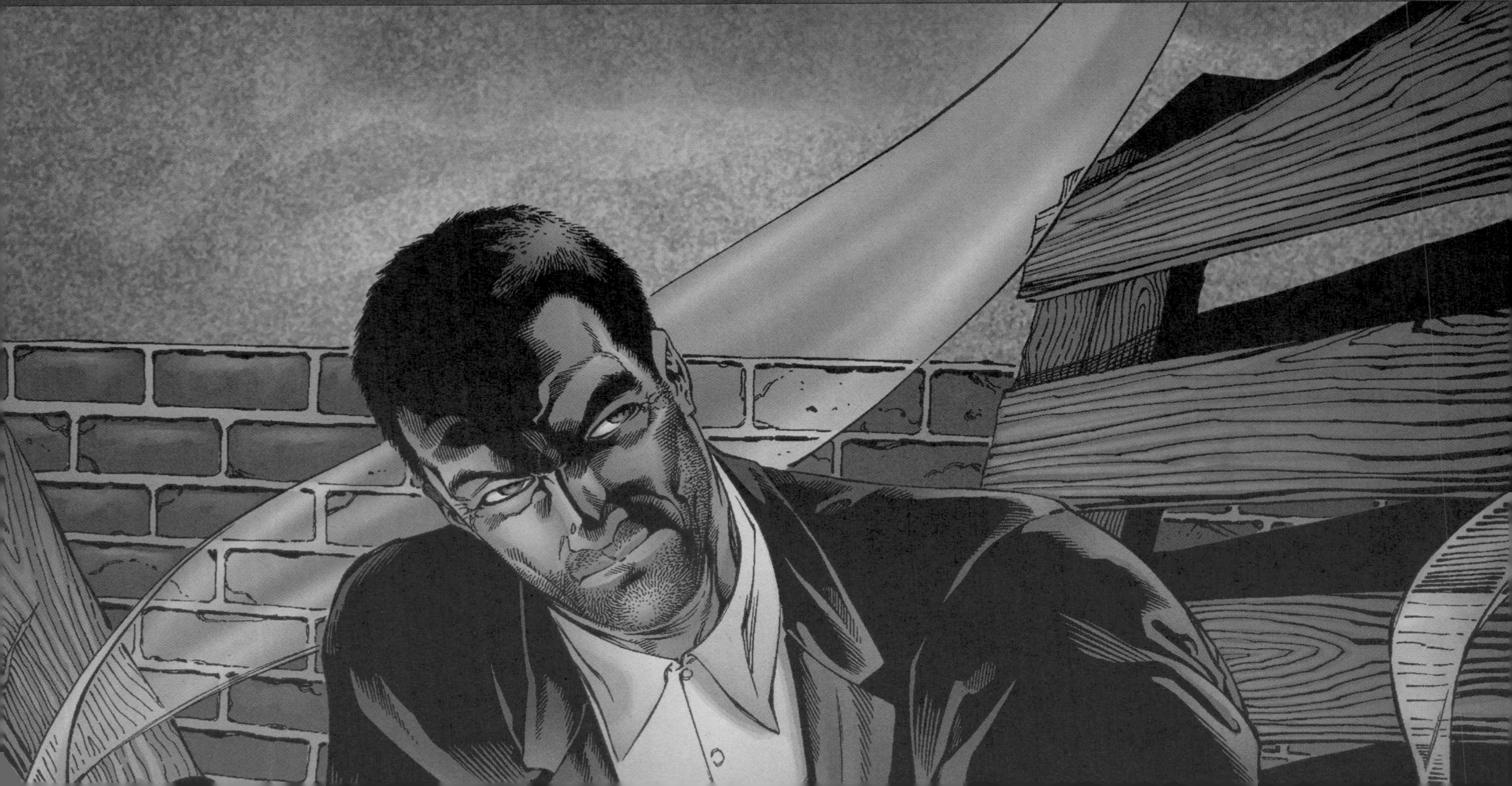

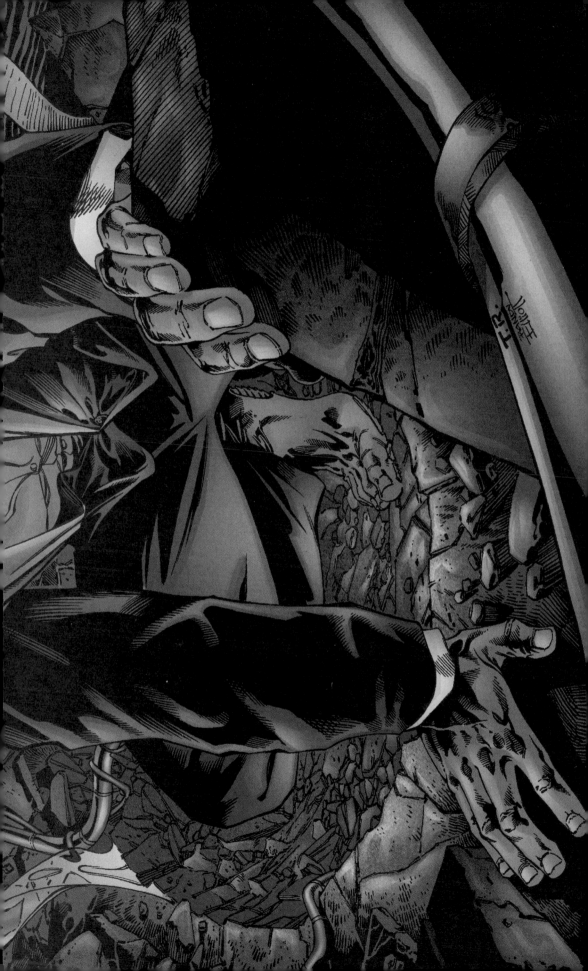

ABEL ETERNITY

UNDYING EVIL

STORMWATCH

No.44 $2.50 $3.60/CAN.

STORM

JANUARY 1997

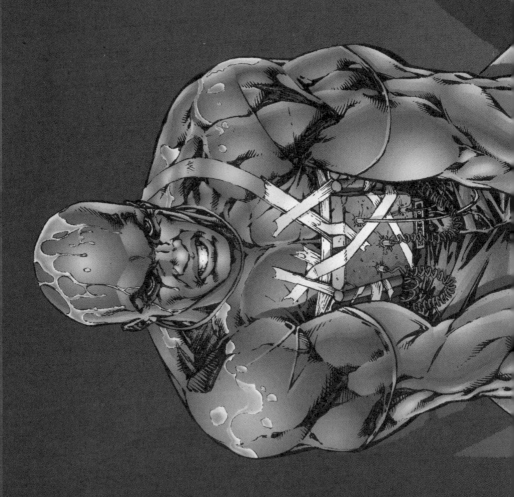

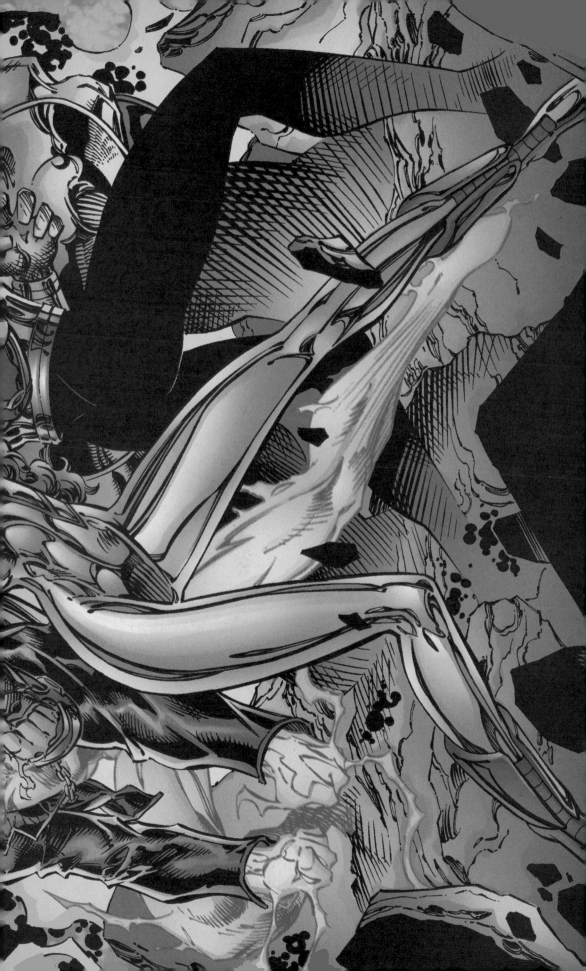

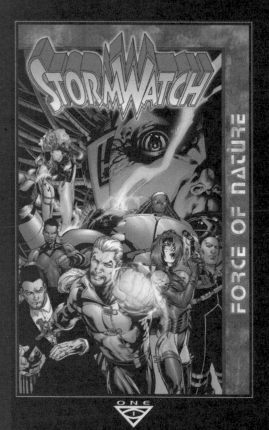

FORCE OF NATURE

ONE 1

LIGHTNING STRIKES

TWO 2

CHANGE OR DIE

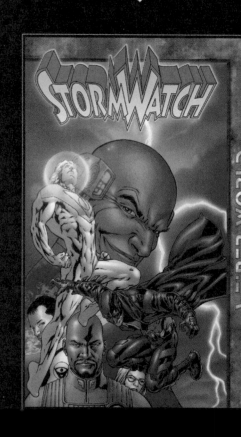

A FINER WORLD

JENETTE KAHN
President & Editor-in-Chief

PAUL LEVITZ
Executive Vice President & Publisher

JIM LEE
Editorial Director - WildStorm

JOHN NEE
VP & General Manager - WildStorm

SCOTT DUNBIER
Group Editor

MIKE HEISLER
MIKE ROCKWITZ
Original Series Editors

ERIC DESANTIS
Collected Edition Editor

RICHARD BRUNING
VP - Creative Director

PATRICK CALDON
VP - Finance & Operations

DOROTHY CROUCH
VP - Licensed Publishing

TERRI CUNNINGHAM
VP - Managing Editor

JOEL EHRLICH
Senior VP - Advertising & Promotions

ALISON GILL
Executive Director - Manufacturing

LILLIAN LASERSON
VP & General Counsel

BOB WAYNE
VP - Direct Sales

MASTHEAD

Look for these other great books from WildStorm and DC:

COLLECTIONS

Crimson: Loyalty & Loss
Augustyn/Ramos/Hope

Crimson: Heaven & Earth
Augustyn/Ramos/Hope

Deathblow: Sinners and Saints
Choi/Lee/Sale/Scott

Danger Girl:
The Dangerous Collection #1-3
Hartnell/Campbell/Garner

Divine Right:
Collected Edition #1-3
Lee/Williams

Gen13
Choi/Lee/Campbell/Garner

Gen13: #13 ABC
Choi/Lee/Campbell/Garner

Gen13: Bootleg Vol. 1
Various writers and artists

Gen13: Grunge the Movie
Warren

Gen13: I Love New York
Arcudi/Frank/Smith

Gen13: Interactive Plus
Various writers and artists

Gen13: Starting Over
Choi/Lee/Campbell/Garner

Gen13: We'll Take Manhattan
Lobdell/Benes/Sibal

Kurt Busiek's Astro City:
Life in the Big City
Busiek/Anderson

Kurt Busiek's Astro City:
Confession
Busiek/Anderson/Blyberg

Kurt Busiek's Astro City:
Family Album
Busiek/Anderson/Blyberg

Kurt Busiek's Astro City:
Tarnished Angel
Busiek/Anderson/Blyberg

Leave It to Chance:
Shaman's Rain
Robinson/Smith

Leave It to Chance:
Trick or Threat
Robinson/Smith/Freeman

Resident Evil Collection One
Various writers and artists

Voodoo: Dancing in the Dark
Moore/Lopez/Rio/Various

Wetworks: Rebirth
Portacio/Choi/Williams

StormWatch: A Finer World
Ellis/Hitch/Neary

StormWatch: Change or Die
Ellis/Raney/Jimenez

StormWatch: Force of Nature
Ellis/Hitch/Neary

WildC.A.T.s: Gang War
Moore/Various

WildC.A.T.s: Gathering of Eagles
Claremont/Lee/Williams

WildC.A.T.s: Homecoming
Moore/Various

WildC.A.T.s/X-Men
Various writers and artists

Wildcats: Street Smart
Lobdell/Charest/Friend

WildStorm Rising
Windsor-Smith/Various

OTHER COLLECTIONS
OF INTEREST

Art of Chiodo
Chiodo

The Batman Adventures:
Mad Love
Dini/Timm

Batman:
The Dark Knight Returns
Miller/Janson/Varley

Batman: Faces
Wagner

Batman: The Killing Joke
Moore/Bolland/Higgins

Batman: Year One
Miller/Mazzucchelli/Lewis

Camelot 3000
Barr/Bolland

The Golden Age
Robinson/Smith

Green Lantern: Emerald Knight
Marz/Dixon/Banks/Various

Green Lantern: Fear Itself
Marz/Parker

JLA: New World Order
Morrison/Porter/Dell

JLA: Rock of Ages
Morrison/Porter/Dell/Various

JLA: Year One
Waid/Augustyn/Kitson

JLA/ WildC.A.T.s
Morrison/Semeiks/Conrad

Justice League of America:
The Nail
Davis/Farmer

Kingdom Come
Waid/Ross

Ronin
Miller

Starman: Sins of the Father
Robinson/Harris/
Von Grawbadger

Starman: Night and Day
Robinson/Harris/
Von Grawbadger

Starman: Times Past
Harris/Jimenez/Weeks/Various

Starman: A Wicked Inclination.
Robinson/Harris/
Von Grawbadger/Various

Watchmen
Moore/Gibbons

For the nearest comics shop
carrying collected editions and
monthly titles from DC Comics
call 1-888-COMIC BOOK.